Three Shorts and a Long

Grandpa's Stories of Wit,
Wisdom, Satire, Humor, and Pathos

Herbert M. Bertram, Jr., M.D.

Illustrations by Barbara Babcock

VANTAGE PRESS
New York

"A Fish for a Lifetime," "Corbet, the Devil and the Ten-pound Bass," "The Legend of Teutonia," "Bobby, Not 'Bonnie,' But Bobby and Clyde," and "The Vanities of Fishermen" reprinted by permission of Sam Piatt of *The Daily Independent* in Ashland, Kentucky.

This is a work of fiction. Any similarity between the names, characters, and places in this book and any persons, living or dead, is purely coincidental.

Cover design by Susan Thomas

FIRST EDITION

All rights reserved, including the right of reproduction in whole or in part in any form.

Copyright © 2001 by Herbert M. Bertram, Jr., M.D.

Published by Vantage Press, Inc.
516 West 34th Street, New York, New York 10001

Manufactured in the United States of America
ISBN: 0-533-13886-8

Library of Congress Catalog Card No.: 01-126331

0 9 8 7 6 5 4 3 2

Contents

Preface vii
Acknowledgments xi

Part I: Factual
A Fish for a Lifetime 3
The Boy and the Buzzard(s) 8
Corbett, the Devil and the Ten-pound Bass 13
How I Gained Aplomb 20
The Flight of the Model A 25
The 1936 Kentucky Derby and My Moment of Fame 28
The Misguided Command 32
The Legend of Teutonia 34
Bobby, Not "Bonnie," But Bobby and Clyde 36

Part II: Fictional
The Great Handicap Flummox (or, "what goes around comes around") by Olivia Ann Massengill 45
The Trivialization of Sports 51
The History of Golf (A Condensed Version) 54
The Vanities of Fishermen 57
A Golfing Christmas Fable 59
The Straw or The Old Man and the Mouse 75
A Message from Dayle 81

Preface

Three Shorts and a Long

The massive rectangular wooden box hung on a wall. In most homes it was near the front door, perhaps because less wiring was required to place it there. As a child, I had to stand on a chair to face the mouthpiece, and to reach the ear piece. The ringing "clanging" was clearly audible throughout most homes.

In small communities, such as mine, there were only "party lines," all connected to a central station, attended twenty-four hours a day by the "operator." Our operators were "Hattie" and "Daisy"—and these two maiden ladies were the heart and soul, the chambers of commerce, the encyclopedias, the Walter Winchells of our town.

One evening, I came home early from a visit to my grandparents. The house was empty, and so I lifted the ear piece, gave a short crank to the ringer handle, and Hattie answered—"Hattie," I asked, (no need to identify—Hattie knew every voice in town)—"Hattie, where's my dad?" "Oh," she said, "he's gone to Mr. Bowman's house to play bridge." Talk about an efficient communication system? Three shorts and a long beats the hell out of Press 1, Press 2, Press 3!

Life was simple, plain, and mostly serene. We fished, we hunted, we went to school, we played football, baseball, and tennis. Evenings, or rainy days, we had great pleasure awaiting, because we read, and read, and read.

By twelve years of age, I was thrilled by Jack London, intrigued by Sax Rohmer, and made happy by "Mark Twain." Bedtime, for me was quite early, and I can recall my father scolding kindly, when he lifted my bed covers at 9:30 P.M. to find me, a flash light and a book underneath.

"Adventure, mystery and humor," Buck, Fu Manchu, and Tom, embodied the essence of what I hoped my life would see. And, they were presented to their audiences in their simplest of language, of word construction; so that they were understandable, rational, or funny to a twelve-year-old or an eighty-year-old. Sadly, so many writers can't seem to do this today.

Before the end of the three shorts and a long era, "Romance" would come along as well, but—that had to wait until I gained aplomb.

Autos were scarce, and there was never a need for traffic lights and almost none for stop signs.

All this existence, bland by today's standards, changed little throughout my childhood.

Oh, there were movies; but black and white, and silent, except for the lady who played the piano, just below the screen. She played gently in romantic scenes, and harshly, tumultuously in scenes of conflict, or storms. Her performances enhanced the images and gave meaning to the events of Mary Pickford and Douglas Fairbanks, or William S. Hart. Looking back, I can believe she had more talent than the stars.

One night I remember three shorts and a long, and when my father answered the telephone, he let the cord dangle, and beckoned me to come listen. When I put the receiver to my ear, there was music—and so, I heard my first radio sounds. Some neighbor had gotten this newfangled device, a radio, and he wanted to thrill all his friends with this marvel. Shortly thereafter we acquired one of these contraptions and I spent a lot of evenings listening to KDKA in Pittsburgh, PA—the only station we could get.

This book recalls the images of my childhood, and some more mature years; it is principally concerned with our most pleasant experience, outdoor life.

Acknowledgments

My thanks to Carolyn Wells, Frances Figart-Brolley, Sam Piatt, and to Barbara Babcock for their kind efforts on my behalf.

Three Shorts and a Long

Part I

Factual

A Fish for a Lifetime

The boy was small, and although nine years of age, he might easily have been mistaken for seven years old. Like many at that age, he was full of misgivings and not entirely without fear in the dark or in unfamiliar settings, and he felt uncomfortable, though not necessarily afraid, when faced with minor physical discomforts, such as briars, or weeds, or cold water or wet clothing.

So it was with some considerable trepidation that the little boy followed his father's instructions. "See that plowed field? Just follow the edge of the creek until you reach the upper end of the field and then walk down the bank to the creek—you'll find the last eddy in Laurel, and a long riffle that leads down here to where we are going to fish in the big round hole—where Laurel empties into Kinniconick. You can't get lost, and if you fish carefully, you might get some nice bass or redeyes."

So off the boy trudged, carefully holding his old rod and reel with a Tandem Spinner snapped to the wire leader, which was the terminal for a spool of eighteen pounds test-braided black silk line.

Unlike later models, the reel had no level wind, and the boy had learned to use the index and second fingers of his left hand to insure a smooth spool, while he cranked in his casts with his right hand. All this was essential to skillful casting, since overlapping of line on spool resulted in a backlash, which resulted in a tangle, and an aborted cast. So, the boy had spent many frustrating hours learning all this,

and having become adept at so doing, he gave little thought to the process.

He gave more thought to the walk along the edge of the field. There were high weeds, tangles of bushes, and briars in the greened area, while walking the newly plowed field, with its uneven terrain caused foot discomfort and balance problems. He worried a little about a chance encounter with a snake, but mostly he was apprehensive because of the uncertainty of the unfamiliar surroundings. His father's reassurances still rang in his ears, but even at such a tender age, he knew that fathers are not infallible. And so he reached the end of the plowed field, and cautiously descended the bank of the creek. The vista that appeared was so beautiful and so appealing that he forgot his fears almost immediately; stretching to his right lay a shimmering lucent pool of clear green water, and to left the pool ended, descending a long riffle with dancing points of light, and a gushing musical sound. The rippling water ran down some thirty or more yards and below this turbulence lay several boulders, which almost encircled a small basin of darker green.

Still on the bank, he began to cast the eddy water: skillfully avoiding the branches, logs, and water lilies, which defined the shore lines. But there were no strikes, and after ten minutes or so, he carefully descended the creek bank an stepped into the shallow water at the head of the riffle. Even though it was May, the water felt icy cold, and his feet were wetly numb—his first thought was to retreat, to avoid this discomfort. Reluctantly, but determinedly, he cast down the riffle; it was shallow and so swift he felt it could not possibly hold any fish; finally, thinking to straighten out any incipient line tangles, he allowed the swift current to pull line off the reel spool, until it was almost all played out. Far down the riffle, just at the entrance to the deep hole below, he saw the sparkle of the spinning blades of his lure, sunlight reflecting from the bait.

Suddenly there seemed to be a flash of white from the pool below, and instantly his rod was bending in an arc, and the pull on his line threatened to take rod reel, line, bait, all from his hands. Then came a great explosion of water as the fish jumped; and now the little boy realized he had hooked a great fish.

The embattled Pisces zigged and zagged, jumped again, splashed and thrashed; the boy hung on for dear life, rod bending, line pulling, reel handle rattling, knuckles bleeding. Slowly he persevered and he fought that gleaming glistening, froth-laden monster up the rushing riffle, until both fish and boy were nearly exhausted. Finally his tremulous body was able to pull the fish into the still waters of the eddy, and thence to drag the flopping creature onto the creek bank.

The fish, however, was imbued with the wisdom of centuries of water-dwelling ancestors. The fish knew where the water was and seemed determined to return to it.

The boy was equally determined that it should not—and so the second stage of the great battle ensued. The fish flounced and flopped and rattled its gill plates, trying to descend the bank. The little boy blocked its descent with hands, and then with feet, and finally with hands, feet, arms and body, scraping up the spine-laden trophy and forcing it farther from the water. By now both were covered with mud, and gravel, and slime, and scales. Slowly, almost balefully it seemed, the fish lay still, with only an occasional twitch or quiver to denote it was still alive. Now the boy used his new pocket knife to cut a branching willow limb, cut off all but an inch of one limb, ran the forked stick up through the gill cover and out the fish's mouth. He hoisted his trophy, and this time he ran across the plowed field, sometimes carrying, sometimes dragging, and triumphantly returned to the Round Hole. Muddled, battered, bruised and bleeding, but grinning from ear to ear, the little boy displayed his catch.

There were congratulatory whoops and cries, and handshakes and hugs. He recounted blow by blow to his father and the fishing friend. The fish was dutifully weighed and measured and pronounced to be of the Esox Maskinonge species. Yes, it was a "Muskie," and 31 inches long and 8 and 1/2 pounds in weight—an elongated winter-thin male, in another month in might have weighed 10 pounds. And it was a fish for a lifetime.

Perhaps the father was aware of the implications of such a great catch for such a small boy. The boy, at that moment certainly was not. But as the years have passed (two-thirds of a century to be exact), and several thousand fish and a few trophies later, I have come to realize that certain valuable truths emerged from that great encounter.

1. Do not be afraid of the unknown. Respect, yes—fear, no.
2. Nothing worthwhile is ever accomplished without some sacrifices—either physical, mental, or material.
3. There is great satisfaction for the mind, the soul, the body, but most of all for self-esteem when you accomplish (even with a lot of luck) what you set out to do.

And so ends the story of "A Fish for a Lifetime" and while I still recognize *some* of the little boy in stressful or challenging situations, I can recognize a *lot* of the little boy when I go fishing.

The Boy and the Buzzard(s)

The hot dry weather of August had arrived and, with it, the beginning of squirrel season. So, the boy carried his sixteen-gauge single barrel to the creek bank, descended the wooden steps from the camp and, as he had done dozen of times during the summer, stepped into the boat to allow the lazy current to carry him down stream. It was very early morning, and the silence was almost absolute. Occasionally a tree frog piped, or a feeding fish made a small splashing sound.

The boy was still small for his age, larger than when he had caught his first muskie, that fish for a lifetime, but not yet the muscular, sturdy youngster who would successfully plead with Corbett not to shoot Devil. He was no longer afraid of the dark, he was now aware that there were two sexes, he had developed an insatiable curiosity, and was an avid reader of fact and fiction. He was totally at ease with his present environment, having spent the preceding three months on or in the creek, fishing, wading, frog hunting, seining minnows, catching craw fish, and tending set lines along the winding shore line. All this was about to change.

The boat drifted slowly downstream. To his right the bank was lower and there was a cleared field, where cattle grazed most of the day. The left and steeper bank was lined with great sycamores, oaks and beech trees, some leaning out over the water where their predecessors lay immersed as sunken logs along the boundary.

The boat came to the first bend of the creek, and he al-

lowed it to drift carefully ashore; silently, he tied it to a small sapling and stepped ashore. Now he was at the foot of a very steep hillside. There was a path, almost a corridor, trampled through the now densely wooded shelf of the base of the hill, where the cows came upstream in the morning and downstream at night to cross the creek to the farmer's barnyard.

Hickories, shag bark and plain, oaks, elms, beeches, walnuts and poplars rose skyward, reaching for sunlight and sustenance, each trying to push branches and leaves above the others.

From his father he had learned that a squirrel hunter must be silent, remain virtually unseen, and listen carefully for the rain-like sounds of nuts being "cut," as the tiny shell particles dropped onto foliage beneath the feeding animal.

Now he heard a squirrel cutting, but when he moved he stepped on a dry dead twig, it cracked, the squirrel jumped to another tree and vanished up the hill before he could even raise his gun. Slowly, very quietly, he moved along the path, creek twenty yards to his left, hillside another twenty yards to the right. The tree canopy seemed ominously high and almost solid, except for a corridor-like opening overlying the ancient cow trail.

Time passed, and he heard no more squirrel activity, so he sat on the moss at the base of a huge beech tree, and waited patiently, as he had been taught to do. Downstream, down the corridor he heard a rustling, almost flapping sound, and by squinting through the foliage he made out a black form, high up in the bleak branches of a dead tree.

It looked like a big crow, as best he could discern; and having watched his father shoot crows he thought it might be appropriate that he test his marksmanship on this old black bird. So he slipped along the path until he could more clearly see the bird, raised his gun, pointed, and fired. To his amazement the bird fell from the tree, plummeted almost to the ground, spread its wings, and swooped sideways, seemed to stall, slipped sideways again, and vanished into the forest. But as it had fallen the bird had emitted an eerie cry, a grunting high pitched rasp, and to the boy an angry sound. By now he had realized that his was not a crow, but a black vulture, commonly called a buzzard.

Still gazing in the direction of the vanished bird, he suddenly became aware that there were noises behind him, and he whirled, to see a great black squadron of vultures, perhaps ten or twelve, wings flapping viciously, flying through the canopy corridor, directly toward him. The lead bird seemed to stare fiercely at the boy. There were hissing sounds, perhaps from wing-air movement, perhaps from malevolent avian vocal cords. Just as the birds passed overhead there came several squishy thuds, and the boy became aware of a horrible odor. The smell was rancid, acrid, and unbelievably repulsive. As he darted to the cover of the nearest tree, he almost stepped into a yellowish brown puddle, which seemed to glisten with a copper stained froth. Frightened, perhaps more than he had ever been before, but by no means subdued, he reloaded the gun and fired in the direction of the departing black vultures. Now he became aware of several more moist brown foul smelling puddles around him. The birds rose above the tree tops, perhaps two hundred yards away, began a circling pattern, as though searching. Their flight was not the lazy, effortless gliding activity he had seen buzzards display before. Rather it was almost frenetic, swift and purposeful. Suddenly the ominous black squadron dove beneath the tree canopy and came charging back down the corridor. The terrified boy, trying to minimize his presence, shrank back against a tree trunk.

The lead bird, he or she, of the baleful eyes, flew directly down the middle of the open space, passing only a dozen feet from the boy, and again there was the sibilant, hissing, air motion sound. Ominously single file, seemingly and endless procession, they flew by the tree where he crouched. After an eternity the last bird passed, but the odor and the malevolence of their passage lingered. Finally, casting all discretion aside, he flew back down the cow path, jumped into the boat, and paddled furiously home to the summer camp.

The memories of the event were to dwell with him for many months to come. Later he learned that this phenomenon, apparently peculiar to vultures, is well know to naturalists. They will regurgitate upon anything or anyone who poses a threat to their existence. Fortunately very few people ever experience or witness such.

Again, as he had when he caught his first muskie, the boy could later realize that he had learned from this experience:

1. Never disturb that which does not concern you.
2. Vengeance is a part of natural order.
3. Never underestimate an adversary, since he may return to dump on you!!!

Corbett, the Devil and the Ten-pound Bass

Prologue

I have never witnessed a homicide, but I almost did so. And even to this day, I shudder to think about what almost happened that fateful day in June 1933.

For reasons long forgotten, my father could not go fishing with his longtime fishing companion this day, and I was elected to take his place. This was somewhat of an honor since Corbett was a very serious and dedicated fisherman, who brooked no nonsense or trivialities when in a fishing boat. So, it meant that I was being treated as an adult, and I hoped I could live up to Corbett's expectations. Certainly I was a proficient caster, and certainly I knew not to move suddenly in a boat, and certainly I knew not to thump the sides or bottom of the boat, and certainly I could paddle without creating noise, or splashes, or touching the wooden sides. A great deal of this proficiency I owed to Devil, since I had watched, practiced, substituted for, and tried to emulate Devil for several years. Devil was a professional guide; taciturn, obliging, a skillful boatman, and very quiet—all the characteristics required for guiding such a dedicated demanding fisherman as Corbett, were embodied in Devil.

When he was third party present, he was called, quite

simply, Devil. When third party absent, however, we sometimes referred to him, no cruelty intended, as The Devil.

I wish I could tell you how he had earned such opprobrium, but here my memory serves me poorly. I do remember, however, what his wages were. Very simply, he required one or two pints of whiskey per day; if there was ever additional recompense involved, I never knew of such. Devil painted houses when there was no demand for his services as a guide. House painting, in those days, was usually a secondary avocation; and there must have been some type of poison in the paint since every house painter I knew required a daily antidote of whiskey.

Corbett was our county clerk, and a very pleasant gentleman. He had the veneer and polish that, it seems, all politicians must assume. In retrospect, I'm inclined to think that the true Corbett only emerged in a fishing boat. He was there to catch fish, by God, and if the fish were not cooperative, his jaw became set, his complexion darkened, and his vocabulary tended toward four-letter words. He was, however, a very skillful fisherman and seldom did he return empty-handed. He had a huge tackle box, which held numerous sizes of Jointed Pike minnows. Tandem spinners, Bucktails, Silver Spoons, and at that particular time a new muskie bait, the Heddon Vamp. Our favorite bait, for then, was a large size Heddon Vamp in a rainbow scale. In this tackle box were pliers, weighing scales, gear grease and oil, extra reels, extra line, and a beautiful automatic target pistol.

Fishing boats, in that era, were all wooden. I'm not sure that the aluminum industry was sufficiently sophisticated as yet, to build the light weight, freely floating, easily maneuverable boats you see today. At any rate, my father and Corbett would probably have eschewed using such a boat, since it was common knowledge that all metal boats were notoriously noisy, and q.e.d., scared the fish away. In keeping with this concept, I can assure you that most of our conversation was only acceptable in a muted, if not whispered, tone.

So, having set the stage, I'll try to tell the story.

The Story

Corbett, Devil, and I set forth to fish Pine Eddy, a noted muskie stronghold. As we turned off old Ky 59, we traversed the tree-lined lane that led to the foot of the eddy, and we passed a cottage with a screened front porch. I remember Corbett mentioning that it belonged to a family from Cincinnati, as he waved to a gentleman in the small yard. Shortly we were in our boat, and Devil was skillfully paddling, ascending the long pool of water. We fished for several hours, caught a couple of undersized bass, raised a small muskie, reached the upper end, and started back down the eddy. About halfway down, there was a cattle feedlot, and the cows had long since trampled away any brush or willows. Most of the banks where we had fished were steep and sharply declining, but here the bank was gently sloping, grassy, with hoof pockets leading into the water. Water lilies in profusion bordered the cul-de-sac, and it was there that Devil announced his intention to go ashore to relieve himself. He adroitly managed his end of the boat to the shoreline and stepped out, pulling the boat ever so slightly ashore. Corbett was in the bow, and I in the middle; Corbett made a short cast to the edge of the lily pads. The Vamp lay on the surface for a brief instant, Corbett twitched his rod tip, and suddenly there was an explosion of sound, water and froth. Now the fish retreated into the water lilies, and as Corbett pulled mightily, the boat broke free of the shore. We were towed, it seemed, to the pads where this leviathan thrashed and struggled. I glanced toward the stern, seeking the paddle, but all the while, reluctant to let my gaze leave the scene of battle. Alas, Devil had taken the paddle ashore, the better to balance his way through all those hoof pockets.

"DEVIL!" yelled Corbett, and now here the Devil came, splashing, stumbling, wading, and swimming, pants half on and half off, portions of his anatomy still exposed.

He grabbed the stern of the boat, and attempted to raise the disheveled dishabille of a personage aboard. The starboard gunwale dipped, water poured in, the tackle box overturned, water came to my ankles, and Corbett continued to pull and fight the hopelessly entangled fish. Finally some semblance of order prevailed, and Devil was able to get aboard, grab the dip net, and with one herculean effort, dip the fish and all the lilies with which it was entwined.

It was a monster of a bass, by several pounds, I reckoned, the largest bass I had ever seen. This was truly a trophy fish, and while still trembling, Corbett managed a smile of relief, even as he too began to appreciate the size of his catch.

"My gawd, what a bass!" he said. "Have you ever seen such a fish, Devil?"

"No, sirree," said Devil, as he ever so efficiently uncapped a pint, and took three rapid swallows. "I'll get 'im on the stringer."

The stringer was of braided metal, and sliding along this strand were some eight or ten oversized sleeved metal safety pins. You unhooked a pin, forced the point through the throat membrane of the fish, closed the pin, attached the metal strand to an oar lock, or exposed railing rib and, presto, the fish was securely strung.

With trembling fingers Devil freed the bait hooks, unhooked a pin, forced it through the fish's throat, out its mouth, closed the pin, and swung the fish overboard to fasten the stringer through an oar lock. Unfortunately the fish, returning to its own element, gave a mighty flounce, tore the stringer from Devil's hand, and vanished.

There was, as they say, a moment of strained silence. I looked at Corbett, and his face grew darker and darker. I looked at Devil; his face grew whiter and whiter. Now there was a mighty commotion, a rattling and fumbling behind me, I looked back at Corbett, just as he withdrew the pistol from the tackle box. Somehow I knew this was not the time for boys to be seen and not heard.

"Wait, Corbett, wait—he couldn't help it!" I shouted back.

Cordell Hull, Dean Rusk, Henry Kissinger all would have been proud of me. I begged, pleaded, implored, almost cried until the darkness began to fade from Corbett's face. I can't remember what I said, but slowly Corbett began to retain his sanity, and Devil his color. I do not remember any further words being spoken until we reached the foot of the eddy, beached the boat, carried our gear to the car, then Corbett spoke again. "Devil," he said, "you can just damn well walk home!"

And he did.

Epilogue

Our great fishing tragedy had taken place on Thursday. Sunday morning, returning from church, my father said, "Mr. Donehoo wants us to come to the grocery store; he's got a fish tale to tell."

And so we walked the length of a block, and entered Donehoo's grocery. This WalMart forerunner was the only emporium that opened on Sunday and then only until noon, so that forgetful housewives could forestall angry husbands, and so that we all could purchase a Sunday paper. Mr. Donehoo was tall, and ever so kind. When my father sent me with a check for our monthly grocery bill, Mr. D. always gave me a sack of chocolates. He was one of my favorite people.

"Had a man in here about a hour ago, wanted to weigh a bass. He was going to catch the ferry, on his way home to Cincinnati. He said he caught this bass, at the bottom of Pine Eddy, just this morning. He said it had a metal stringer hooked through its lip."

"How much did it weigh?" I blurted this out, before my father could ask.

"Weighed seven pounds eight ounces, and it had already been gutted, too."

I'll leave the reader to figure out how much that great fish must have weighed, before spending three days dragging a heavy stringer, and before it was disemboweled. I'd guess ten pounds, maybe more; but all this pales when I think of the homicide I almost witnessed.

The next day Devil told me, from the top of a ladder, that he had caught a ride home, and the guy had sold him a quart of "shine."

The next Sunday, Corbett, my dad, and Devil went fishing. I was happy for the Devil. Having been, again, consigned to the nether regions, he was being permitted to return.

How I Gained Aplomb

Prologue

Aplomb, to the current generation, is an archaic word. Today's youth, by high school age, has already gained a degree of sophistication and self-assurance that came to my generation only through some meaningful event, or events; and then only at an age far past puberty. My generation grew up in an era of innocence and as this tale unfolds, the reader, hopefully, will understand what I'm attempting to say.

The Story

Roy and Sallie came to our town in the early thirties, from a tiny hamlet some thirty miles south. This town was probably, by numerical size, the equal to ours, but it did not have the magnificent sweeping Ohio River bend. It did not have Alum Rock, nor the Hanging Tree. It did not have the only monument to the Union Soldier south of the Mason Dixon line. Therefore, we considered it to be a lesser community.

Roy was a lawyer and by some reports a mischief maker, to put it kindly. There were rumors he liked to drink. "Miss Sallie" was genteel, and gracious, and in Roy's presence somewhat obsequious, to put it kindly.

And so it came about, in my sixteenth summer, that "Miss Sallie's" niece, from the lesser community, came to visit her aunt (and perforce, her uncle as well). Shortly thereafter I received an invitation to come to their summer camp, on lower Kinniconick, to meet this young lady and to bring my swimming trunks.

My father, the distinguished local physician, had no problem in handing me the keys to his car. Nor do I remember any sage words of advice about my conduct for that lovely moonlight evening. It was assumed, I presume, that having been taught good manners, I would do nothing to embarrass my parents.

The drive was only some seven or eight miles, and when I arrived, I was greeted by a very convivial Roy, and a more subdued but equally gracious "Miss Sallie." I was pleased to be so warmly received, but the intensity of my pleasure grew by leaps and bounds when I was introduced to the niece, Miss Julie. She was, indeed a lovely young lady, slightly shy, but overwhelmingly beautiful of face and form.

"Miss Sallie" had prepared a meal of fried chicken, cream gravy, corn on the cob, fresh tomatoes, and hot biscuits. We all ate with gusto. I did not put my elbows on the table (although Roy did), and I carefully thanked my hostess, and her helper, Miss Julie, for such a splendid repast.

Miss Sallie suggested a game of Rook, but Roy, who had grown more convivial after two trips to the bedroom, insisted that Julie and I must take a "moonlight boat ride and a swim."

So, I was led to Roy's bedroom, where I got into my swimming gear, and then I politely led Miss Julie down the steep steps from the camp to the creek bank. Miss Julie had by now gotten into her bathing suit. (Hugh Hefner was an unknown at that time but, in retrospect, the impact would have done justice to his future publications).

There was an old John boat, with oars and oat locks, which pleased me as I was a proficient rower. Julie would sit on the stern facing me, and she would then be exposed to the magnificent biceps and chest muscles of her companion. (After all, I subconsciously thought, Miss Julie wasn't the only prize in this boat. I'm sure that was a subconscious thought since, along with good manners, I had been taught not to brag).

Above me I heard Miss Sallie say, "Roy!" in a reprimanding voice.

I was about to cast off when Roy stumbled down the steps and handed me a blanket and a small jar (I must have gotten to midstream before I began to wonder what they were for).

Resting on the oars, I somewhat surreptitiously opened the jar. Its size and shape suggested my grandmother's treatment for chest colds. I smelled; it was slightly musty, but there was no menthol present, as far as I could tell. I tested it with an index finger. It was some type of lubricant, I thought: Maybe the oar locks needed greasing? No, there were no squeaks as I pulled us out into midstream.

The brilliant moonlight here made a sharp contrast to the subdued light under the tree-shore canopy. Frogs bellowed, crickets shrieked. Fireflies beckoned, and we ascended the eddy as I pulled manfully on the oars.

Midway up there was a nice gravel sandbar on one shore. We glided to this bar and stepped ashore. Julie tested the water with her toes—"Oh, my," she said, "it's cold. Let's just sit here and listen." So, I placed the old blanket on the smoothest area of the bar, and we sat. Shortly thereafter we were reclining, and the so-smooth skin of her shoulders was atop my outstretched arm. I knew, again subconsciously, that something was about to happen. I felt certain that it was up to me to make it happen, but still dwelling in the age of innocence, I knew not what.

Suddenly there came a revelation—I gently pushed her shoulder straps down. She did not resist. Emboldened and inspired I took out Roy's jar, and using second and third fingers of my right hand "au pair," with savoir-faire and great aplomb, I rubbed the Vaseline on her chest.

Epilogue

Days passed, but I never understood why Julie did not call or write. Maybe she didn't understand or appreciate true aplomb.

The Flight of the Model A

The first thing I believe about young drivers, as opposed to older more experienced drivers, is that: they think one, they're invincible; two, that speed is the solution to any problem; three, that seat belts will keep them safe. All three of these premises are false and all young drivers should be taught not to rely on any of them.

I think I started driving when I was twelve. I might have been thirteen, but in those days if you could reach the pedals, see over the wheel, and you had access to an automobile, you drove. Sometimes with "parental permission," sometimes, if you could manage it, without such.

I must have been fourteen or early in my fifteenth year when my father, one summer Sunday, left with Mr. Corbett Knapp to fish an eddy on Kinney. He told me that if I wished to come join them, once Sunday school was over, I could use his car, a 1930 Ford Model A coupe with rumble seat, to get to where they were.

So, I sat in the back of the ME South Church, skipped out the door as soon as my class adjourned, ran one block home, got my fishing rod, hopped in the Model A and took off at a daring twenty-five miles per hour. Up Vanceburg Hill, down Rock Run Road to Tannery, turned right and soon got near what was then "Mr. Cook's Camp," and the fishing eddy for the day.

I was less than half a mile from where I wanted to go, traveling the one lane road with very high shoulders on each side, when I rounded a slight bend and almost ran head-on into an old Model T sedan loaded with Saturday night revelers who "kept on comin'!" I slammed on the brakes, and even as unsophisticated as I was at that early age, it only took me a moment to realize that they weren't going to stop, let alone back up.

They waved and cheered, and I waved back, feebly—I couldn't see anything to cheer about. In retrospect there might have been a metal personality clash here. Lest that statement be considered inane, consider the fact we love some autos and detest others. The clutch-grinding, gear-scratching, brake squealing of high performance cars is highly appealing to some and an abhorrence to others. Some of today's drivers may find the smooth gliding of an automatic transmission far more appealing than the gear-shifting, clutch-lifting of hot rods. As some great person once said, "To each his own." Let's face it, all autos have personalities. But enough philosophy, let us return to the scene of the confrontation. Certainly no self-respecting T, even if guided by human hands, was going to give Rights of Passage to an upstart A.

I jammed the gear in reverse and trying my best too steer while looking out the back window, I rocked and rolled about one hundred yards backwards, where, thank goodness, the six-foot high shoulder on my left side diminished to about three feet. I turned the steering wheel and the backend went left, I gunned the motor, and by golly, the whole coupe popped up onto that bank.

My oncoming adversaries flew by with cheers and waves of a few bottles, left a cloud of dust, and disappeared down the road. I finally walked the last half mile and found my father—needless to say both he and Mr. Knapp were dumbfounded when they saw how I had positioned the Model A. The undercarriage was completely on the ground;

the right front wheel and the left rear wheel were hopelessly dangling in midair.

To make a long story short, one hour and one team of nearby horses later, the car was back on the road, apparently none the worse for wear.

My father was one of the kindest men I have ever known and most certainly one of the bravest. He let me drive home, and he rode with me.

The 1936 Kentucky Derby
and
My Moment of Fame

This Saturday eyes and ears of the world will again focus on our glorious Commonwealth because at about 5:00 P.M. Saturday, the Kentucky Derby would be run. This has to rank among the top five sporting events of all time, and for horse racing it's #1, the most prestigious of all races.

I know sometimes you are not interested in my reminiscing, but let me tell you that I first attended the Kentucky Derby in 1936 and therein lies a story. Because in 1936 there wasn't a lot of money floating around, and we were just beginning to emerge from the Great Depression and almost all college kids, of which I was one at that time, didn't have the wherewithal, so to speak, to attend horse races, let alone bet on such. Well, to tell the truth fairly, neither did I.

I was ending my freshman year at the University of Kentucky, and for the life of me, I can't tell you why I decided to go to Louisville to see the Derby, but I did.

First there was a matter of finances. Well, somehow from my monthly $40 allowance, I had saved $5. That really wasn't that bad since, at that time, Cokes were a nickel and hamburgers were sometimes as much as ten cents and we could buy a meal ticket for a week's time on campus restaurants for something less than $5.00.

Secondly, there was a matter of transportation. Well, by city bus, a dime took me to the end of the line at Versailles Road. I got off at the end of the line and stuck out my thumb.

So it's 1936 and hitchhiking was easy. Very few people turned down hitchhikers in those days since mugging, highjacking, and petty thievery were almost nonexistent. If you had a car and were going somewhere, you helped the less fortunate. You didn't need to worry if some hitchhiker was going to harm you or steal your money. It was that simple and two car rides later I caught a man and his wife on their way to Churchill Downs. Voila!

Well, they ever so kindly deposited me at the backside of the track and for fifty cents I got to scramble across the track and into the infield. The infield was far different then compared to how you must know it from television now. There weren't naked people running around, there wasn't a lot of booze floating freely about, and there weren't any drunks as far as I can remember.

I must have reached the Downs somewhere around eleven or twelve o'clock in the morning. For the next four and one half hours, I wandered about the infield, talked to a few people, vaguely watched horses circling the track as the other races were going on, heard the crowd yelling and managed to acquire a paper that told me more than I could understand.

At some point in time, I guess it dawned on me that people came to bet on those things, something I hadn't even thought about. I had come to see the Derby. But by late afternoon the inside rail of the track was solid people, and I was about to despair at finding any kind of vantage point where I could see even the finish line, much less watch a bunch of horses run all the way around the track.

The finish line was completely obscured from any viewpoint from the infield by a large wooden building. On each side of the wooden building was a large hedge encircled by a fence, which extended out for some distance on either side. The finish line was apparently just opposite this wooden building. On the backside of this building was pure white wood, no windows, two stories tall; there were no ledges and nothing to permit an ascension, so to speak. But, wait a minute, along one corner of the building, there was a slender drainpipe coming down one end.

Well, the bugles blared, the crowd's rumbling grew louder, and the loud speaker announced the names of the horses as they approached the track, and I went up that pipe, all thirty feet of it, hand over hand, legs dangling, until I reached the roof. Somehow I got one leg up over the roof and on the gently sloping surface. I gave one last heave and, behold; I was on the roof. It sloped upward slightly and so I walked gently up some fifteen feet and, lo and behold, I had the best seat in all of Churchill Downs.

There were a cadre of officials, and perhaps, twenty state troopers in the enclave below, which I now recognized as the winners circle. There, after the race, the winning horse would be brought to receive his collar of roses.

When I reached the front edge of the roof and stuck my feet over, my appearance caused quite a stir in the people who were seated facing me around the grandstand and the clubhouse. At first the state troopers couldn't understand what the commotion was all about. Finally one of them looked up and then the commotion really began. They sort of scattered around right and left looking for a way to come and get me, and there wasn't any. Finally one of the troopers loudly commanded me to "come down"—and I commanded him to "come and get me."

The Derby entries were strung out to my right up the track, preparing to enter the starting gate. People waved at me, cheering. I waved back and gave the state trooper a somewhat taunting salute. I had the best seat in the house, but suddenly I heard a footstep behind me. At first only one, and then over the next five minutes, there were many, many as more and more agile young men were able to make their way up the pipe as well. They also realized there was a ringside seat up there atop the tote board building and it was there for the taking. Soon this building, which apparently was not too sturdy to start with, began to rock and sway as the load on the roof far exceeded what it had been designed to carry.

My perch, which had been secure, was now precarious and the roof top was oscillating, so to speak, as more and more men tried to get forward and get a clear view of the entire race and the finish line.

The crowd roared as the horses left the starting gate, and I hung on to the front edge of the roof hoping the whole thing wouldn't collapse and deliver me to those troopers standing down below.

I did see the entire race, and I clearly saw the finish. I watched all the elaborate presentations that ensued. I didn't get to make a bet, I had no idea what horse won, I didn't know who owned the horse or who the jockey was, but I did see the 1936 Kentucky Derby, start to finish. And everybody who was there saw me.

The Misguided Command

In retrospect I would like to share another recollection of Churchill Downs. This time with only an audience of a few hundred people. But again, I inadvertently became the center of attention by committing a dumb mistake.

It was May of 1942, I was a medical student and we were all, as medical students, enlisted in the student program of the Army ROTC or the Army Medical Reserve Officers Training Program. In other words, we were in the Army. Of course we must not forget that a few of our students were in the Navy.

By virtue of the fact that I had only recently completed about three years of military training at the U.S. Naval Academy at Annapolis, and I knew most of the military commands, and presumably knew left from right, I was elected as company commander of the U of L (University of Louisville) student medical corps. As I recall there were about 300 medical students in our company and most of the men (there were also two women) had had no previous military experience. So I assumed command of this group.

Somehow we were asked to make a public appearance at Churchill Downs during this spring meet. Once we arrived I managed to march my company south on Fourth Street until I reached the street that led directly to Churchill Downs, where a right turn would put us at the entrance. From there we would march proudly into the Downs, an example for all to see of our dedicated service men and women who would soon be actively engaged in the great conflict of World War II.

As we moved into the center of the street, I gave the command: "Company, left turn!" "March!" My well-trained cadre of would-be soldiers executed brilliantly and turned left; only now we were marching away from Churchill Downs.

Well, the only true soldier present (and he was marching alongside) was my commander, a U.S. Army Sergeant Major who had been entrusted with the training of these "raw" recruits, and this was the man who had selected me to be company commander. To say the very least, he was "whizzed" off.

Out of the corner of my eye, I could see his expression and he was about to have a fit. Here was the result of all his efforts and endeavors for the past six months marching the wrong way by 180 degrees in front of several hundred civilian spectators.

He was about to take over command of the whole misguided outfit when my brain suddenly kicked into high gear. Well, how do you turn a hundred-foot long train completely around on a narrow track? Simple. With great aplomb, without a bat of an eye, I boomed the command: "Company, halt!" "About, face!" "Forward march!" So we entered Churchill Downs with great military precision.

However, like a lot of people who were subsequently in the Pentagon, I never let on I had planned anything different.

The Legend of Teutonia

In northeastern Kentucky, in the county of Lewis, there is legendary stream, Kinniconick. This stream bisects Lewis County, running almost fifty miles from south to north, to empty into the Ohio River. Kinniconick has been a world-famous muskie stream for two centuries. It winds, it twists, it flows through a long-wooded canyon that drains the hills of Lewis County, the fifth largest of Kentucky's one hundred-twenty counties. Near the midsection of this stream, there is an island, perhaps six acres in size, and the only island on "Kinney," as the locals call it.

In the late 1800s, a group of prominent citizens from the county seat, Vanceburg, acquired the island and formed a club whose members were accorded visiting rights. These men were well educated, pillars of their community, church going, and well respected, conservative citizens.

Ostensibly, the purpose of the club was to have a communal meeting place, enhanced by the fact that it was several hours journey by horse and buggy, in a very sparsely populated section of the county. There they could meet and discourse or debate upon matters of great import for their community, the state, and the nation.

Presumably there was a Franco-Prussian, Germanic ancestry here, since they chose the name "Teutonia." It may have been coincidental that the sparkling waters of the stream were loaded with redeyes, bass, and muskellauge, so the members, when they were not pondering affairs of state, could cast a line. And of course, when their minds were tired after hours of debate and discourse, they had need for some form of recreation in the evenings. So, the great round table where they pondered and discussed all weighty matters, had little bins facing each seat where they could place important documents or other necessities for pleasure as the evening progressed.

Sometimes around the Great Table controversies would arise, but these were usually settled amicably by parliamentary procedure and the rules of a man named Hoyle.

Food, of course, was a necessity, and the club employed a full-time general "factotum," a Mr. John Morgan, whose job was to feed this distinguished group of statesmen. And so, there came a day when supplies were running low, and one of the officers of the club, a Judge Pugh said, "John, you'd best go to town tomorrow and get some supplies!"

The next morning, Mr. Morgan hitched horses to wagon and departed. By late daylight he had not returned, and some members were concerned. After all, it was only a thirty-mile round trip, and surely he should be back. All members were well into the afternoon session when the clanging, splashing sounds of a wagon crossing the creek were heard. And so they all placed their important papers face down upon the table, rushed out, and descended the sloping creek bank to meet Mr. Morgan.

"John," asked Judge Pugh, "what have you got?"

"I got two barrels of whiskey and a sack of flour, suh."

Whereupon a Mr. Hammond, widely known for his ability to get at the heart of any weighty matter, very gruffly shouted, "What in the hell did you get all that flour for!"

Legend has it that Judge Pugh then snapped, "Shut up, Lewis, after four nights and three days of poker and liquid refreshments, I believe I'd like a biscuit."

Bobby, Not "Bonnie,"
But Bobby and Clyde

To really appreciate the nuances, and perhaps the hidden motives, behind this story, it is necessary to have some background information on its participants. So let me explain that neither Bobby nor Clyde has ever met a stranger. Both of the protagonists, and possibly antagonists, have very warm, exuberant, outgoing personalities. But there their similarity ends.

Bobby is country boy, smooth, a born horse, mule, and knife trader. He might have been a politician, but basically, he is far too honest and while he has been known to equivocate on occasion, most of what he says you can write down as the truth.

Clyde is equally charming, Texas-entrepreneur style. He can tell more entertaining stories in an hour than Danielle Steele has written, complete with details as to who did what to whom. He has been all over the world and is on a first-name basis with a lot of famous people. It would take a Dan Jenkins to truly portray the flavor of Clyde's personality but there must to be football coaches in the Southwest Conference who have patterned themselves after Clyde.

Bobby has this easygoing, inquisitive manner that makes people want to lie on his couch, figuratively, and to spill forth details that they probably wouldn't disclose to their closest friends. Recently he and I were hunting on a large expanse of very private property when a uniformed guard suddenly appeared to check our credentials. Bobby

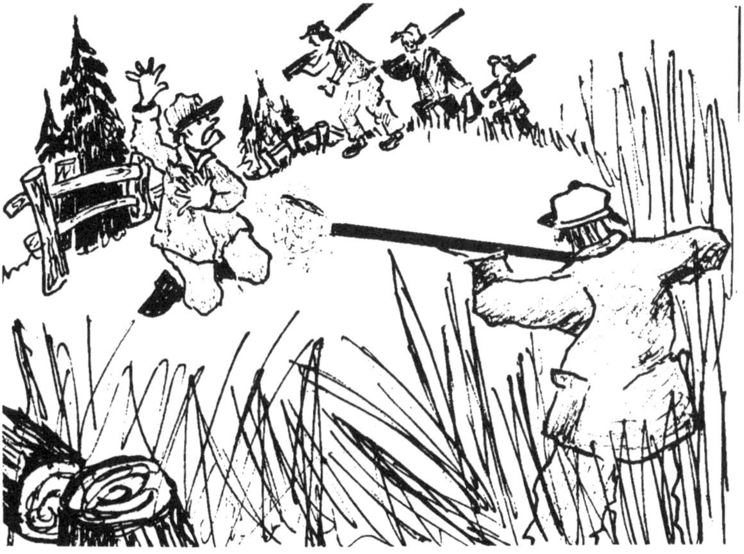

spent three or four minutes speaking with this man. Shortly thereafter he told me the guard's name, where he lived, how many children he had, how many miles a day he drove, and the man's hourly wage. Had I asked he would probably have known the guy's favorite food—needless to say, I didn't ask. Clyde, on the other hand, would probably have known all these things even before meeting the guard.

Despite their similarities, and their differences, Bobby and Clyde were the closest of friends, blood brothers, so to speak, and each very willing to forgive any transgressions from the other.

And so we went quail hunting, taking several of our boys, on a sunny November day. Each member of this group had his own favorite shotgun, but for this discussion, the only gun of note was that borne by Bobby. It has to be the ugliest gun ever created by man; a Browning automatic, .12-gauge. It weighed slightly less than a full garbage can, and to my mind, was about as appealing. To make matters worse, affixed to the end of the barrel was this unsightly bulge, an appendage that is called a Poly-choke.

Twist the dial one way, and it is alleged to create an open choke; twist it in the opposite direction and the choke is full. For the uninitiated or uninformed, all shotguns have a choke. The last inch or two of the interior of the barrel has been machined to promote spreading or condensing of the shot pattern as it leaves the barrel. An open choke spreads the shot, whereas a full choke keeps the shot in a tighter pattern. The maximum effective range of a shotgun varies with the type or size of the shot, the choke of the gun, and the load, or grams of powder in the shell. Theoretically a .28-gauge shotgun will shoot just as far as a .12-gauge; but it delivers fewer pellets to the target. I would guess that a .12-gauge, .28-inch barrel gun loaded with number 8 shot would have a maximum range of approximately 100 to 120 yards, depending upon the pointing azimuth. The effective range, however, is considerably less. I do know that many times I have been sprinkled with falling shot, which was fired from over 100 to 120 yards away. But it is like a gentle rain and does not puncture clothing or skin. My personal preference lay in a simplified design, and a smaller gauge gun, but Bobby liked his .12-gauge monstrosity, and shot extremely well with it. He shot far better than I, on most days, so any note of disdain I might have conveyed might better be interpreted as envy—but I diverge, so, on with the story.

We had flushed a covey, and the birds had flown perhaps 200 yards across a small ravine, to spread out and alight in some sparse bushy cover. Bobby and my son, Mike, elected to follow, hoping to flush the singles. We watched from the gentle sloping hillside, as a bird flushed, and flew almost directly at us. Bobby raised his gun and fired; the bird plummeted to the ground. Clyde said, exuberantly, almost jubilantly, "That rascal just shot me!"

The exuberance I could understand—Clyde was exuberant in all things. The jubilation I could not understand (even though I now do). It was almost as though he was preparing to say "My lawyers are Bailey, Ketchem and Tweedle." Bobby, completely unaware of the misery his life would hold for the ensuing weeks, picked up the dead bird, stuffed it into the hunting coat, and proceeded through the distant brush tailing the other singles. Now Clyde *Carpe diem*'d, shouting as though in great agony, "I've been shot!", and slumped to the ground, holding his right hand against his chest, rocking back and forth. I've seen better performance in a senior play, but like every role Clyde played in life, he played it to the hilt.

Now Bobby came running, hunting pants rubbing to generate that peculiar grunting swishy sound only hunting pants can generate. His usual open-faced smile was replaced with dark concern; and apologies spewed forth. Clyde accepted these with all the graciousness of feudal lord, forgiving a miscreant vassal.

Being the only *"tenems"* in this *"locum,"* I inspected the wound; Clyde's hands were thick skinned from years of corporate paper shuffling and bird house building, and this was a most fortunate happenstance, since I could scarcely find the puncture mark. There might have been a tiny drop of blood beneath the epidermis, but barely so, and lodged in the dermal layer was this very clearly visible minute black spherical object.

In my best hillside manner, I made the diagnosis; somehow sensing, but not really knowing all the implications. "Clyde," I said gravely, "you've been shot." Inane, yes, but I didn't know what else to say.

"Well," said Clyde in the brave manner of a true Texan, "why don't you squeeze the dern thing out, and we'll go on hunting."

I was trained, at least in part, in battlefield surgery, but my hands were not particularly clean, and the only surgical instrument available, in this moment of crisis, was a Barlow that Bobby had traded for two days before. Since it had come from a Fleming County framer, I felt it had a high potential for harboring tetanus spores. So I demurred, saying, "I'll get it out when we go by the office going home."

"Must have been that darned high brass," mused Bobby to no one in particular, "nothing else would make my gun carry that far." We all nodded in agreement that it was nearly impossible for a pellet to reach such a distance with enough force to inflict a wound.

"Shot my old rabbit dog once," said Clyde, "and he was way off, but I had high-powered shells and number 6 shot."

Things returned almost to normal on the way home.

We laughed and joked, and Clyde was his usual exuberant charming self. He told some stories about hunting in Mexico and flying into a part of Arabia to deliver baksheesh to an oil potentate. Our *esprit de corps* seem to be restored.

In my office it took only a couple of minutes to wash the wound, prepare the site of the incision, nick the overlying thin layer of skin, and pop out the offending pellet. No anesthesia was required, and Clyde the Stoic was restored to his former state of euphoric health (*All's well that ends well*, I thought, but then I've never been known as a thinker.) A spot Band-Aid covered the wound, and my friends departed.

The remainder of the story is strictly second hand. My correspondence in the community where Bobby and Clyde reside gave me regular dispatches of rumors that went something like this:

1. Clyde was gravely ill, after suffering a gunshot wound to the head.
2. Clyde's doctor had advised against amputation.
3. Bobby was despondent and considering psychiatric care.
4. Bobby had shot Clyde in a fit of jealous rage.
5. Clyde had stabbed Bobby in retaliation, with a dirty Barlow knife.
6. Bobby had been served a citation by the State Police for possession of an illegal firearm.
7. Clyde was in daily communication with Bailey, Ketchem, and Tweedle.
8. Some of Clyde's neighbors had offered Bobby a better job.
9. Some of Bobby's neighbors had offered to testify on Clyde's behalf.

10. Bobby's wife and Clyde's wife were seen shopping together, purchasing identical sleeping tents and sleeping bags.
11. Residents of Lexington Avenue reported campers in Central Park.
12. And last, and the only rumor I believed—Bobby and Clyde had gone to Lake Erie together to fish for walleyes.

In truth, they did go, and Clyde overturned their boat, and Bobby almost drowned, but that's another story.

Twenty years have passed, and they are, indeed, the best of friends. Still my heart sometimes aches for Bobby, who will forever be known as "that man who shot his best friend."

Part II

Fictional

The Great Handicap Flummox
(or, "what goes around comes around")
by Olivia Ann Massengill

"Julia Dawn Hobstetter was unanimously elected chairperson of the Annual Women's Invitational Golf Tourney, scheduled for July 13," excerpt from the *Country Club News,* 18 June 1987.

Everybody knew Julia Dawn would be chairperson. She always is. Don't ask me why. Maybe because her sidekick, Portia Ellen Funsterwald, always nominated her, and then Elvina Duke Mayfield seconds the nomination, and then Portia Ellen makes a motion, the nominations cease, and then Elvina Duke seconds the motion, and then we vote. And so it went, right on schedule, as it always does.

Julia Dawn was her usual, reticent, stomp-on-anybody self.

"Everybody knows those women from Rosemont, and Maystown, and Huntingsville always come in here with false handicaps, and take home all our trophies! Well, they're not going to do that this year, or my name isn't Julia Dawn Hobstetter!"

"How do we do that?" asked Peggy Finch, timorously. We are always timorous when we dare to question Julia Dawn. I could hear several of the girls gasping.

"Everybody knows my son-in-law, Gerald, keeps the computer handicaps. This year I'm going to have him factor in the course ratings from our course, along with the course ratings from all the other courses. We'll raise our handicaps by five or eight strokes. Then we'll take our teams from the most improved players. They don't know some of our new players, so they can't complain if Lottie Mae or Mary Sue have 32 handicaps."

Lottie Mae had shot a 44 on the back nine yesterday. Mary Sue had played college golf, but after having three babies and a four-year layoff, was just rounding back into form. Mary Sue is really a sweet person. She can't help it if her husband is oversexed.

"Everybody," said Julia Dawn (when Julia Dawn says "everybody," everybody listens, just like E. F. Hutton), "everybody will have a job to do, and I want you all to do it, and follow the schedule sI have made out for you!"

Last year, I remembered, she hadn't made a schedule. Little Barbara Madden, who comes to our meetings but only plays nine holes a week, had been placed in charge of ice. The tournament was scheduled for mid-July. Poor thing was so flustered at being given such an important job that she filled up her garage with ice in June.

To no one's surprise, Julia Dawn had already compiled her committee lists. I was in charge of keeping score. My husband is an accountant; therefore, by Julia Dawn's reasoning, I was the ideal person for such. Peggy Finch was in charge of Rules and Decisions. Her husband is an attorney. Margaret Mason was in charge of decorating. Her husband is an interior decorator and a wimp. Food and beverages went to Lucy Forrest Youngblood. Her husband runs a catering service and, rumors say, massage parlors. Prizes and trophies went to Evelyn Elstadt. I couldn't figure that out, since her husband doesn't do anything. My husband says he's a bagman for the Mafia. Just joking, of course. She drives a Mercedes 450 SL, and her license plate says HERS I, his BMW plate says "MINE." I've heard rumors they have separate bedrooms. And so it went. I'll say this for Julia Dawn, she runs a hell of a tournament, and runs and runs!

Sunday, July 13 was hot. We committee people all had straw boaters with "WAIT 87" in red letters on blue headbands. Mine was two sizes big, and it kept flopping over my eyes when I bent forward, or falling off when I looked up. Julia Dawn had presented these, as favors, to us at our last pretournament meeting. Her husband runs a haberdashery, and I made a mental note to check the financial statement for the tourney, to find out how much he had charged us. Fat chance, I thought. Her friend Elvina Duke is Finance Chairman.

Little Barbara Madden showed up in halter and shorts. Julia Dawn sent her home to change. She came back in high heels, earrings, and a pink linen suit. She looked scrumptious. Julia Dawn said, "Take off those high heels, or else don't go near the greens!" Poor thing. She went barefoot the rest of the day.

Merilu Morgan and Fannie Craycraft were supposed to measure closest to the pin or number four. They're both so damn nearsighted they can't even see the pin, let alone read a tape measure. Julia Dawn gave 'em a seeing eye—one of the boys out of the caddy room. The service cart carrying drinks and sandwiches to numbers six and fourteen turned over going down the hill on five. Joyce Bergman fell out and broke her left arm, but she didn't tell anyone until she finally fainted, an hour later. I guess she didn't want to upset Julia Dawn.

We finally got all the players teed off by 10:45, and while there was a lull, I went to the john. I could hear some of the other girls talking in the locker room.

Peggy asked, "What's the penalty for hitting a putt twice with the same stroke?"

"Who did that?" someone asked.

"I did, the other day—and I asked Lee. He said, 'Was anyone looking?' "

The other person said, "Ain't that just like a lawyer?"

Peggy giggled, then pretended to be offended. "I'll have you know Lee is a stickler for rules. He knows so many he can find a rule to overrule a rule."

The other girl said, "Sounds like what John Hatcher told Lee Ann the other morning. She had to let him in the house about 7:00 A.M., 'cause she had bolted the door. He says, 'I couldn't get in, so I slept in the hammock.' She says, 'I gave that damn hammock to the Salvation Army three weeks ago.' He says, 'That's my story and I'm stickin' to it!" John is a lawyer, too.

I went back to the scoreboard. The first group was coming up nine. Just about that time this huge black cloud came over the hill behind the clubhouse. I got the first three foursomes on the board before the lightning and thunder started. It rained, on and off, the rest of the day. Most of the scorecards were indecipherable, but that didn't faze Julia Dawn. She read off the scores. I just put 'em on the board. When we were through, Lottie Mae had won low net by two shots, and some girl from Huntingsville was second.

The breast of chicken with almonds and raisin sauce was cold; my salad was wilted. I excused myself, sneaked into the bar, and had a double martini, very dry. Some of the men were there.

"You girls have fun today?" one asked.

"I think I want a second opinion," I said.

"Gladly," he said.

"Just kidding," I said. "We had a barrel full, a barrel full."

"I'll buy you another," he said.

"No thanks," I said. He was cute, but not that cute.

I could hear Mary Ann Burchett, our president, who is truly a lady, and she was making her little speech.

"We so enjoyed having all you nice people here. We look forward to inviting your clubs, and sincerely thank you for your participation." There was applause, and the meeting broke up.

I almost forgot to tell you. Lottie Mae's scores had read 5-6-5-9-6-etc.

When Julia Dawn came to the "9," she cleared her throat and said, "How'd that nine get in there?"

The lady from Huntingsville said, "She hit it in the water."

"Was she first on the tee?" asked the lady.

"Well," said J.D., "we have a local rule—the Hobstetter rule. It reads 'The third player of a foursome with a handicap of 32 or greater, whose ball shall enter the hazard on number four hole, shall be deemed to have a free drop, at no penalty."

"She hit her second ball and third ball in the water, as well," said the lady.

Lottie Mae was standing there. She corrected them. "I was second on the tee, Julia Dawn."

Humph," said Julie Dawn. "You didn't let me finish the rule. It further says, 'The second player of a foursome, with a handicap of 32 or greater, whose ball shall enter the hazard on number four hole, or whose succeeding balls shall enter the hazard on number four hole, shall be deemed to have four free drops at no penalty.' So you were on the green with your fourth ball, and two-putted. You had a three."

"I'd like to see that in writing," said the lady from Huntingsville.

"I'll mail you a copy," snapped Julia Dawn, adding, "we will score this tournament strictly by the rules, as long as I am chairperson."

I'm only glad she didn't say chairwoman.

I went to the locker room, just as they were all leaving. I overheard the lady from Huntingsville say, "I'm gonna send her a collar and a case of Alpo!"

Oh, well, I thought, we'll get the same treatment when we go to their courses. Everyone knows what goes around comes around.

Libby Massengill

The Trivialization of Sports

If one sought common denominators to tie together all of this world's inhabitants, then we might think of food, shelter, and procreation, and rightly so. In the U.S.A., however, for the most part, we expect (and receive) these things as our birthright. They come because our birth certificate says we were born in Podunk Center, Podunk County, Podunk State, U.S.A.

Our parents own land, homes and businesses, which we inherit, trade, promote; and sometimes lose. That's okay, too, since this is the land of opportunity, and we go out and earn more land, homes and businesses. We are able to do this because our parents saw that we were educated to do it; and because everybody's gain is somebody's loss; or conversely, everybody's loss is someone's gain. This happens every day and, collectively, we give it little thought. Individually, we may suffer or rejoice, depending upon whether we gave or received.

There is an area of human endeavor in the U.S.A., however, where we all collectively (redundant, I know) gain, in enjoyment, every day of every year. We call this *Sports.*

Sports, because of television, and radio, and newsprint, and books, and participation, affects our lives to a degree that is almost unimaginable.

Try (briefly because this is an exercise in futility) to imagine that all sports have been banned in the U.S.A. Suddenly, TV programming is cut to six hours a day, newspapers are only eight pages in size, radio reverts to replays of Jack Benny and Amos and Andy; all sports magazines (including swimsuit issues) disappear, and you sit in your living room gazing wistfully at your Ping iron, at your Head racquet, or your graphite spinning rod. Since the only sport now permissible must take place in bedrooms, the world population zooms, food and energy supplies are soon exhausted, and we revert to cave dwelling, from whence we came thousands of years ago. Oversimplification, you may say. A bit, perhaps, but only the time frame is uncertain. The rest seem inevitable in this fantasy.

There does seem to be one bright ray of hope in this scenario. The population explosion might be lessened by the ever-increasing numbers of homicides, fratricides, matricides, and suicides that ennui would spawn. Even AIDS might become popular.

(But we'd better not count on it.)

All of the above must lead us to an inescapable conclusion. We are nothing without *Sport*. Amen.

But (and it is this "but" that demands attention) somewhere along the line, in the ever-expanding national obsession with *Sports*, we seem to have lost sight of the meaning of the word. The concept of sport as fun, as a mentally-enriching, spiritually-awakening, self-satisfying experience has gone down the drain. Only in the sports that are purely self-participatory pursuits does some fun still remain. All the others have been demoted to a less-than-meaningful state by satiation. The media overexposure of the N.F.L., the N.B.A. and all the other alphabetized sports leagues has left us with the blahs.

Sadly, this satiation, which, by itself, might be almost tolerable, is now compounded by trivialization. Who wishes to know, or even cares, what third baseman took a called third strike in the third inning of the third game of the 1983 World Series? Or what tennis star called the linesman a son-of-a-bitch at Wimbledon in the fourth set of the Davis

Cup matches in 1976? Or John Madden's hat size? Or how many times Billy Martin has been ejected for spitting on an umpire? Or how much tobacco is chewed by the major league players on a given day?

But statistics and the recall of absurdities are now served to us daily in indigestible masses by the ever proliferating modes of "Sports" information. For two weeks prior to the Super Bowl, we were inundated and overwhelmed with minutiae. No detail of the public and private lives of the participants was overlooked. Everything was covered, from the color of Doug Williams's shorts to the presence of trichophyton on the locker room floors. If we must have trivia, why cannot it evoke more interesting images?

So, enough with the microdot information yet. Let's get back to basics. Think how refreshing a news item would have been had it read:

San Diego, January 29th.
 The Washington Redskins defeated the Denver Broncos 46–10 today, to win the Super Bowl.
 During the second quarter, when Washington scored 35 points, a ravishing blonde spectator removed all of her clothing. The lady's husband left in disgust. Only one other person noticed, a disgruntled, five foot, four inch ex-reporter from the *Chicago New Tribune.* He had been fired after the '87 Super Bowl for failing to report in millimeters the exact size of the part in William Perry's teeth. Later, to other spectators, this man reported the lady's measurements as 40-26-36, with an interareolar distance of an astonishing sixteen inches. Airport authorities say a short man in a gray snap-brim felt hat, and a buxom, scantily-clad, light-haired woman boarded Delta Flight 807 to Las Vegas. Departure was at 9:14 P.M., with an ETA of 10:32 P.M. in Vegas.

Now that's readable *Sports* trivia!

The History of Golf
(A Condensed Version)

Is it possible that you are not aware that golf was almost stillborn, or that it barely survived infancy? The facts are that the game, or at least its rudiments, emerged in Scotland in the thirteenth century. (1) By 1457, the game became such a national pastime to the Scottish youth that it was about to supplant archery as their "tour de force." Since the archers were the first line of defense for the British Isles, this could not be allowed to continue. In 1457, Parliament issued an edict, banning golf. (Imagine an infantry division armed with drivers or mashie niblicks. This would certainly not intimidate an invading horde of Huns, Visigoths, or Vikings.)

As you can predict, this led to surreptitious action, not unlike the effects of our own Volstead Act, by landowners and the peasantry. It spawned scenarios that were to be repeated in America in the 1920s, and even later (do you watch "Miami Vice"?) and it coined some phrases that only achieved full significance five centuries later.*

TIS an hour pre-dawn on the seacoast of Scotland in the year 1459. A gangly youth stumbles in semi-darkness along the seastrand, straining to see the bulk of the headland, perhaps thirty feet higher. He sees motion, and the grasses part upon the moor above.

---

*From Winslow's *An Irreverent History of Golf,* 340 pp., Invain Press, Parchment-Illuminated L500-hard cover—$29.95.

"Who goes there?" comes a whisper from above.

"Aye, and it's me, Angus McGillicuddy. Are you the keeper of the goff?"

"Speak easy, lad, the goff wardens are about. What do you wish? And speak easy, mon."

"I've come to try a wee spot of goff. How do I get up there?"

Now a dimly lit lantern is held in his view, and the keeper says, "I'll turn up this light, and y'can see yon path the better."

"Aye, that's better. Hold the lantern higher, and beam me up, Scottie!"

Emerging upon the plateau above the beach, Angus is met by the keeper.

The keeper says, "I can see yer clubbies, but where are yer featheries, mon? Ya nae kin play the golf wi'out featheries."

"Oh, I've got 'em in the leg of me boot," and so the term "bootleg," was aborn!

"Well, ye ken play at earliest light, but that will be happence, to be paid in advance."

Not unlike the modern game, green fees were a burden, even then. No doubt the keeper had a nice selection of midirons and feather-stuffed balls, as well, all available at bargain prices.

In 1490, an event occurred that now overshadows what was to happen three thousand miles west and two years later. Historians have paid little attention to the former, and made much fun of the latter, which only goes to show how truly unperceptive historians can be. King James IV, or maybe it was James II—my memory is a little vague here—took up, as they say, goff. From that day forward, the Edict of 1457 was ignored. To hell with the Visigoths and the Huns. Let 'em invade. The king has a nine o'clock tee time!

This event also took golf out of the horny hands of the peasantry and placed it squarely in the palms of the aristocracy, with the Vardon grip, of course. There it remained, virtually, until the ascendancy of Arnold Palmer. He gave it back to the troops and, in so doing, earned our undying gratitude.

(*Webster's Unabridged* does not acknowledge these sources of some of the terms above, which only goes to show that Webster could be unperceptive, too!)

Root Canal City

There was a golfing dentist, from
Upper Molar, Texas,
A might swing adventist, he.
His golf ball hit him the
Solar Plexus
By rebounding from the marker of the tee.
While lying on the ground, writhing around
He was queried as to the cause of his plight.
Gasping for air, with only a slight
vacant stare,
Said he, "I think I shall turn my
Left hand slightly to the right."

The Vanities of Fishermen

Fishing can be a sport, an avocation, an occupation, an obsession, a frustration, a physical challenge, and a financial strain. It sometimes does all these things simultaneously, thereby placing a great strain upon man's well-being. We all know that man has evolved from some lesser form, and presumably fish have done the same. Such evolution has resulted in a challenge of the species.

That famous fisherman, Izaak Walton (1563–1633), set the standards when he penned *The Compleat Angler*, and his influence has bedeviled mankind ever since: He died penniless and may have been the original Alzheimer. Strangely, today, literally millions of men are still trying to emulate his way of life, thereby placing great stress upon the medical, legal, and financial worlds. There seems to be no greater challenge for a fisherman than bass fishing. Broken homes, physical debilitation, and bankruptcy are common among bass fishermen.

Oh, the thrill of hooking a big bass! The pulling, tugging, splashing, thrashing, jerking, pulling, tugging, splashing, thrashing, yanking, jerking, pulling, tugging, splashing, thrashing! What great exhilaration comes to man as the monster is lifted aboard!

Loud cries of exhilaration, congratulatory slapping of hands, sighs of relief, and the sense of a magnificent accomplishment! And so there *are* great rewards from bass fishing. Perhaps Izaak Walton said it best when he wrote "Good company and good discourse are true sinews of virtue."

In summation let us say, "We hold this truth to be self-evident,

>Man is smarter than Bass,
>*Sometimes.*"

A Golfing Christmas Fable

Partridge and Peartree
or Jack and Jill—Up the Marital Hill

The following is from the *Atlanta Post Journal* of December 27, 1989. "Partridge—Peartree." "A candlelight service on Christmas Day at the Buckhead Baptist Church solemnized the union of Jill Partridge, daughter of Mr. and Mrs. Robert Partridge of Atlanta, and Mr. John Peartree, son of Mr. and Mrs. John Martin Peartree of Seminole, Florida.

"Mrs. Peartree has been employed in the brokerage firm of Partridge, Jackson and Lee. She is a graduate of Rollins College and the Wharton School of Finance.

"Mr. Peartree is a partner in the architectural firm of Wright, Mossberger and Wheat. He is currently in charge of the Buckhead office.

"The bride and groom departed for a wedding trip to Miami, following a reception given by the bride's parents at the Country Club of Atlanta."

Act I

Scene I   6:00 P.M., JUNE 21
              A Bar and Restaurant
              Peachtree Street
              Atlanta, Georgia

Jack Peartree was dark, handsome, and an avid golfer. Locker rooms around town were replete with stories about his physique and charm. Stopping at a Peachtree bar to assuage a thirst, on an evening in late June, he was smitten by a gorgeous blonde at a nearby table. She was busily chatting with three other girls, flashing a smile that reflected several thousand dollars of orthodontistry.

"Hey, Dave," he asked the bartender, "who is that little blonde number by the window?"

The bartender answered, "Ya' got me, pal, but if she is still here when I get off at 9:00, I'm going to find out!"

H'mm," muttered Jack, "how about another draft while I go to the men's room?" He arose from the bar, walked to the table where the girls were seated, and with his most polished manner spoke to the blonde. "Pardon me, but are you Sara Morrison?"

"No—I'm not," she replied in a polite but definite fashion. The tone was soft, and she did not seem offended, but there was a positive note that seemed to say, "I've heard this line before."

Jack continued, "I'm sorry to intrude this way, but my secretary's sister was supposed to meet me here—I've never seen her, only know that she is a good-looking blonde."

One of the other girls, a petite brunette, spoke, "Hey, will I do?"

Jack grinned, and for the light-haired girl, it was like a flash of lightning. Almost apologetically, he said, "Gee—I sure hope she doesn't show up! Can I sit a spell and buy you a round."

Several weeks later, Jill Partridge met Jack's secretary and inadvertently found that she, the secretary, had neither kith nor kin. The subject was never mentioned further, but Jill filed a memo in her mind.

A whirlwind courtship zoomed, and the striking couple became frequent sights at discos, clubs, and restaurants about town.

They were out on only their second date when Jack said, "Jill, I'm really a golf nut—I guess I'd better tell you now—'cause if we keep seeing each other, I'd want you to play golf with me, and maybe you wouldn't like to do that."

She replied, "Oh, I understand about being a golf nut—my father is a golf nut—after all, 'golf is a form of mental disorder,' to quote Kenny Lee Puckett!"

"Kenny Lee Puckett," he said. "Who's he?"

"Kenny Lee was the protagonist," she said.

Jack interrupted, "Protagonist, sounds like a prize fighter—only Kenny Lee I ever knew as from Chinatown in San Francisco."

"Oh, Jack," she replied, exasperated. "Why must you talk like a red neck!"

"Ecumenical," said Jack.

"What about Ecumenical?" she asked.

He grinned. "You called me a 'red neck,' made me think of Ole Bubba Henry—one of our defensive linemen"—he paused, thinking back.

"And what's with the Ecumenical bit?" she asked.

Jack explained, "Well, Ole Bubba was a mite slow, great big guy, good natured, but mean as a snake on the field—he needed a snap course, and signed up for a one-hour lecture in theology. As far as we could tell, that word was the only thing he got out of the course, but he sure got a lot of mileage out of it. He got so he had a one-word vocabulary. If he didn't like you, or what you said, it became an epithet—just the first two syllables—say them."

"Ecu," she said, then paused with her mouth open.

"See what I mean," said Jack with almost a vulgar profanity, "now try the rest."

"Menical," she said.

"That's what he used to denote a meaningful phrase or statement, or that he understood what you said. When he wanted a superlative, he used the entire word. "See that slam dunk—ecumenical, man!" Or maybe a big car wreck—'ecumenical!' He could drink beer and listen to stories all night using that one word as his contribution to the rap session."

"Oh—ecumenical!" she said.

"Right on, baby," said Jack, "and don't be putting me down about being a Red neck."

"Menical," she said. Then she thought a bit, "Well, I'm a little rusty, but I can play golf. I'll talk to Daddy tonight and maybe we can play at the club tomorrow. Anyway, Kenny was the protagonist in Dan Jenkins's novel, *Dead Solid Perfect*."

"Oh, that Kenny Lee Puckett. What else did he say?" questioned Jack.

Jill said, "Well, he said, or I think he said, 'Golf is like life, there comes a time to fish or cut bait.'"

"Menical," he said.

Act II

Scene I   1:00 P.M.—June 22nd
           The Country Club of Atlanta

Jack Peartree was indeed a golf nut. A 4 handicapper, he was long off the tee, sometimes wild and erratic, but like his idol, Arnie, he scored well by scrambling out of trouble. He was slightly apprehensive on the first tee, hooked his tee shot badly, and wound up with a double bogey. Then he went par, birdie, par. Meanwhile, Jill was topping her tee shots, whiffed one in the fairway, looked up on every shot, and continued to smile. She complimented Jack on his length and his ability to scramble out of trouble. He refrained from giving advice until the fifth hole, a 150-yard par three over the water. From the ladies tee only about 130, an easy iron to a forward sloping green.

"Jill," he said, "maybe you could do a little better if you didn't over swing and tried a little harder to keep your head down."

"Oh, Jack," she said, "I really appreciate you trying to help me." Whereupon she put the club back past parallel, moved on the shot, and sculled it into the water. Sighing, but still smiling, she placed another ball on the front of the tee, skipped this one across the water where it rolled up the bank an onto the green. Jack took a full swing with an 8 iron, sliced the ball out over the pound where it turned miraculously in mid air, hit the left front, rolled sharply right and went in the hole.

"Oh, my goodness!" said Jill. Jack jumped straight up and whopped and gave his impression of a Mardi Gras reveler. Calming down slightly, he lifted Jill off her feet, swirled her about, and planted a firm and lengthy kiss upon her parted lips.

"Hey, baby, how about that!!" he exclaimed. "My first hole in one." Jill was apparently as ecstatic as he and congratulated him warmly. The rest of the round was almost anti-climatic. Jack, pumped up, continued to scramble for pars, chipped in for a birdie on eighteen and finished with a neat 70. Jill, seemingly, was content to bask in his glory, and finished with a vainglorious 120.

"I think you're lucky for me, Jill, let's do this again on Thursday, at my club," he insisted over dinner. She seemed somewhat reluctant at first, but she finally agreed.

Thursday, on the first tee, Jack appeared anxious to improve Jill's game. He rearranged her grip, spread her stance slightly, and talked about such things as casting at the top, pronation, supination, leading with the hips, lateral movement, firm left side, and visualizing every shot before the swing. He gave her a lesson on alignment, head cocking, wiggle, waggle, sand play and club selection. Had he been more observant, he might have noticed a certain tightness along her jaw line and an occasional tremble of the chin, but he was determined that she play better, as might be fitting for the wife of a scratch golfer (which he intended that she and he become, respectively). Jill shot another 120.

That evening as she passed the den at home, her father asked, "Well, how did it go today, kitten?"

"I don't know if I can do this or not, Daddy."

"Hang in there, kid, I'm betting on you."

The weeks passed, and terms of endearment grew greater between Jack and Jill. Finally, he popped the question, over a candlelight dinner, in late September. "Honey, I think you are the greatest thing to come into my life since my first set of Ping irons. Will you marry me?"

Suppressing the urge to make a Molotov Cocktail out of the wine bottle and his tie (which bore little crossed drivers embossed in gold on a navy blue background), she sighed, beamed joyfully, and exclaimed, "I thought you'd never ask—I will, I will, I will!"

Scene II   The Partridge Home in Atlanta

Now nuptial plans were made, remade, and remade. He wanted to be married on the first tee at her club; he in plus-fours and she in short skirt. Her father vetoed that, vehemently. She wanted to be married in a quiet, family-only ceremony in the rectory of her church. Her mother vetoed that vehemently.

Finally, after several days of discussion, taking into account their jobs, vacations permissible, and their names (which had Yuletide connotations), they agreed upon a ceremonious wedding, in full formal attire, with all the attendant pomp and circumstance. Said wedding to take place on Christmas Day, with honeymoon at Doral.

Now showers were given, teas attended, out-of-town guests invited, in-town guests invited, relatives invited, rehearsal dinner and reception planned and arranged. Gifts arrived by the dozens upon dozens, and the prospective bride and groom went through a whirlwind of parties. Two bedrooms of Jill's home had to be set aside for all the benevolent benefits being heaped upon the lovely couple. Almost nightly, Jack was forced to accompany Jill as she opened the day's treasure trove. Being a neat scribe, it became his chore to log in each article in the Bride's Book, being careful to record the proper name of the item, and correctly spell the name of the donor, with full address for the thank-you notes.

"One dozen wine glasses, from Mr. & Mrs. Robert E. Lee," Jack said.

"No, those are goblets, and crystal, dear," Jill replied.

"Six silver spoons from Dr. and Mrs. Edelveiss?"

"No, those are sterling silver serving spoons," and so it went.

"Hot dawg," he said, "now here's a gift that makes some sense for a change—how about this—it's a videotape 'Golf for Ladies,' with a playing lesson by A.I.M. Shepyard—who the hell is A. I. M. Shepyard—sounds like a border collie—never heard of him—anyway, can we look at it?"

Nervously, she said, "No, dear—it's bad luck to use any wedding present before the marriage. Just record it, and put it on the table with all the other stuff." Dutifully he obliged, but he made a mental note that this was one gift he intended to view at the earliest opportunity.

Scene III   The Atlanta Post Newsroom

The bachelor party went well, the marriage ceremony was very impressive, and the reception was gala and elegant. The bride and groom arrived at Doral in the early morning hours of December 26.

The very next day an article appeared on the society columnist page in the *Atlanta Post Journal*. It read:

> The Holiday Season in Atlanta has been at its most meaningful style this year with the wedding of a Partridge and a Peartree. Jill Partridge was married to John Peartree on Christmas Day. The bride and groom are both well known in Junior League circles. The wedding was a lovely affair and they have departed for Miami and a golfing honeymoon.
>
> Jill Partridge is well known in Georgia as the three-time winner of the Georgia Ladies Open. She played on the golf team at Rollins College and was named to first team All American her senior year when she led her team to a resounding victory in the NCAA golfing Finals at Ponte Vedra, Florida. Graduating Summa Cum Laude in econom-

ics from Rollins, she later obtained a Masters in Business Administration from the Wharton School of Finance. She has joined her father in the brokerage firm of Partridge, Jackson and Lee.

Jack Peartree, a rising architect in the firm of Wright, Mossberger and Wheat, is the grandson of an Olympic decathlon medalist of 1924, John Osceola Peartree, who later became nominal chief of the Seminole Tribe. Jack's father, Lieutenant General (Ret.), U.S.A., John Martin Peartree was the highest ranking U.S. Army Officer of Indian descent. Jack Peartree was a first-string quarterback for Wake Forest, guiding the Deacons to a 34–12 victory over Oklahoma in the Sugar Bowl in his senior year. Fortunately, Jack also plays golf, and is ranked as a low-handicap player at the Stone Mountain Country Club. Jack made a nationally syndicated gossip column two years ago when he was asked by the State Department to escort a jet-set personality during her visit to this country. Sexy, voluptuous, the Maharani of Jodhpur, Princess Farana was shown local bistros and nightspots during a three-day whirlwind tour of Atlanta. Our informants report a very, very good time was had by all.

Appearing on a local talk TV show, in the week following the Maharani's visit, Jack got himself into a bit of local hot water when asked what impressed him most about Farana. He casually mentioned that he hadn't heard a single "You'all" during the three days. He also praised Farana's wardrobe, including unmentionables, a statement that raised the eyebrows of more than one local belle.

Scene IV 8:00 A.M.—December 27th
The Robert Partridge Home in Atlanta

Reading the morning paper over coffee, Mr. Robert Partridge reads this item in the local gossip column, looks at Mrs. Partridge, and says "Jumpin' Jesus!"

We have now set the stage for you (metaphorically), and the curtain is about to rise on what was almost (but not quite) the final act.

Act III

Scene I Noon, in the bridal suite, at Doral, Miami, Florida. December 27th

Jack slowly opened his eyes, slightly displaced in time and location, finally recognizing the darkened suite. He languidly pushed sheets aside, felt for Jill, sat up, looked about and realized she was gone. They had been in this room for almost thirty-six hours and these had been the most satisfying, enchanting, and erotic thirty-six hours of his entire life. He felt a sense of loss so keen he could scarcely believe the sensation. Where was his bride? He wandered to his unpacked suitcase. Probing, groping for clean underwear, his hand encountered a smooth rectangular box. *What the hell is this?* he thought as he pulled the object from underneath a sweater and held it to the dim light from the heavily curtained windows. Oh, that videotape he had purloined from all the mess of silver, china, linens, appliances on exhibit at Jill's parent's home. He hastily dialed room service, hung up, showered, shaved, and emerged from the bathroom just in time to help the bell captain hook the VCR to the room TV. Tipping the bell captain, he inserted the tape and sat back to enjoy the golf lesson promised by the title.

Scene II   Same Place—thirty minutes later

The door rattles, opens, and Jill enters, dressed in golfing attire, with newspaper and purse under her arm.

"Where the hell have you been?" snaps Jack.

Taken aback, she mumbles, "Oh, out and about." Then responding to his tone, she said, "What the hell do you mean, asking me where the hell I've been?"

Sheepishly, apologetically, little boyishly, he says, "I missed you!" Then, remembering what he was angry about, asked, "Well, where the hell *have* you been?"

The answer came back in like tone, "I've been out to see a man!"

"Hey, wait a minute—we're on our honeymoon, and you sneak out of our nuptial bed, as they say, to go see another man—I don't believe this!"

"Well, you'd better believe it, and I didn't sneak out, I just left without disturbing your snoring, and I may see him again tonight!"

"Snoring! Wait a minute, lady. I don't snore!"

"The groundskeeper must be cutting down the palm trees around the waterfall then, 'cause what I heard was either a chainsaw or the sound of a glutted, rutted male named Jack Peartree!"

This gave him pause, but only for an instant. "Well, I'm pissed anyway—if there's one thing I can't stand, it's a deceitful woman!"

"How dare you!" She couldn't think of a suitable expletive, so she stomped her foot, ran to the bathroom and slammed the door.

Sensing that he had the enemy on the run, so to speak, hoping to maintain the initiative (but not quite certain he would want the consequences), he shouted through the door, "I saw the great lady golfer, Jill Partridge, on TV. Hah!

And what's this about seeing him again tonight? Over my dead body you will!" There was a pause, the bathroom door opened ever so slightly, he heard his first marital sniffle, and all the starch suddenly left his spine. "Jill, honey, I'm sorry. I just couldn't believe my eyes when I watched that tape. Here you are on camera, and that nice old gentleman tells about how good you are, and all the tournaments you have won, and here I see your gorgeous swing, watch your little fanny wiggle for all the world to see and I thought about how you deceived me into thinking you had a 36 handicap, when all along you could play like that!" He paused, "Well, anyway, I just got mad as hell!"

Jill emerged, ran to his arms, seeking reassurance that he was going to forgive. "Honey, I promised my daddy I wouldn't beat you on the golf course—at first it was hard not to, but as the summer went on, I fell in love, and the harder I tried to play, the worse I got!! It wasn't all deceit—and I love you too much to ever hurt you." So—they embraced and one little thing led to another little thing and soon they were fully unclothed and back on the bed.

Jack soon found, however, that the stamina that made him a Peachtree legend was slowly deserting certain portions of his anatomy. This time the lovemaking was over in about fifteen minutes. Hands underhead, Jill's smiling face on his chest, he suddenly thought of something. "Hold it, lady—you snookered me! What about the other man?"

"What about the other man? What about that luscious tidbit, Princess Pirahana or whatever her name is!"

"Hey, that happened two years ago, that's none of your business, and her name is Farana." He was just one decibel below a shout, and his face was getting red.

"Oh, yeah—well, I'm making it my business; and while we're at it, why didn't you tell me you were a hotshot football player and that your grandfather was a Seminole chieftain? And what about old Pirahana's matching bra and panty sets you bragged about on TV? I'm sure they came off easily. Tell me, when you'all and Pirahana got together, did you'all sire any more royalty?"

"Hey, you," he shouted, "that's in the past, and I've never asked about who you bedded before me—and quit saying 'you'all,' dammit!"

"I never 'bedded' anybody, you insufferable son of a Seminole." She got this out just before she let go of the heavy monogrammed ash tray. It flew past Jack's ear and lodged past the draperies covering the balcony window. "And I know somebody I'm not about to bed again either!"

The passing Japanese golfer, in the cart below did not, as reported later by the *National Inquirer,* sustain as a "Lacerated Gluteus Maximus on the Golf Course." In the first place, he was not on the course proper, merely on the cart path below. Secondly, the laceration from the glass shard, was to the seat of his polyester pants with only the merest nick of his posterior skin. His worst injury was "loss of face," so to speak, and having to abide with the giggles of his comrades, who, for the rest of the excursion referred to him as "Cut-Butt San." Unknowingly he was to exact revenge upon Jack and Jill some fourteen holes later. Fortunately, the whole event was ascribed to an errant golf ball, thus saving our protagonists (to whom we now return) the necessity of explaining a broken window. Jack, having successfully dodged the ashtray, wishing to end the inquisition, said in a small voice, "How did you come by all this sudden knowledge about me?"

"It's all right here in the Atlanta paper—I got the paper so I could read about a certain marriage that may not last another thirty minutes, that's how!—and while I'm at it, let me tell you about your golf game—that hole-in-one you had was about the biggest fluke I ever saw—I'd be ashamed to claim it! You've got a bad habit of laying it off the line at the top, your back swing is way too fast, your grip stinks, and you look up on every damn putt; other than that, you're no worse than a lot of other Don Juans I've known!" She paused, out of breath.

"Oh, so you've known a lot of Don Juans. Well, what about the one you went to see this morning?"

She giggled and said, "Oh, he's quite handsome, very rugged, has great hands." She paused for this to sink in, then quietly said, "He's only eighty-seven years old, too!"

Somewhat mollified, Jack asked, "Who is he?"

"My old instructor and the finest gentleman of his time, Angus Ian McPherson Shepyard! He teaches here at Doral."

"Oh, the old guy in the tape."

"That's my man, Jack, and you'll love him—but I got to warn you, he gave me a lesson this morning and I'm back in form. I'm going to take you out to the Blue Monster this afternoon and beat your butt." Which she did, and with the aid of a certain Japanese tourist, put them both on national TV.

On the first tee of the Blue Monster, Jack, still inwardly seething, demanded, and received four shots, since she was a scratch golfer, and he still carried a 4 handicap. He knew he was in for the battle of his life, golf-wise, and was determined not to be completely humiliated. Jill, having made her brag, had her jaw set and was equally determined that the family golfing title would once and for all be placed in distaff hands.

We will spare you details, but they went into 17 tied in match play, Jill four shots up by medal. Jack watched in horror and disbelief as her second shot hit a palm to the right of the green, ricocheted left and rolled to a stop about six inches from the pin. Fuming, he hit his second shot, dead at the pin, but a little low in trajectory, it hit the pin and bounced sideways, ending in the fringe thirty feet away. She had a tap-in birdie, while he could manage only par.

Furiously, he gunned the cart toward the eighteenth tee, arriving just as a group of Oriental-appearing gentlemen were ready to tee off. The epitome of golfing courtesy, these smiling, bowing, gentlemen, by gestures insisted the twosome play through.

Jack, still furious over the treatment accounted him by the Fickle Finger of Fate, insisted Jill hit first and she proceeded to the ladies markers. One of the Japanese gentlemen, displaying a miniature video cam, seemed to wish to photograph the tee off. Jack nodded acquiescence, little knowing that would place him and Jill on the evening news. He did note that this particular man had a peculiar rent in the back of his trousers.

Jill, classic swing in the groove, belted her best drive of the day; dead center, far from the lake that runs completely along the left of number 18.

Jack, still unnerved, took a mighty swing and topped the ball, which went dribbling out east by northeast, stopping about a yard from the bank of the lake.

Muttering imprecations, he jammed the pedal to the metal, slowed to allow Jill to jump aboard, and leaving the cart path at full speed, headed for his ball. Old "Cut-Butt San" got the whole thing on film. It showed the cart whizzing across the fairway, showed Jack ferociously stomping on the failed brake, showed the plunge off the bank, showed the great shower of water, showed the emergence of the two mud-splattered dripping golfers, even showed Jill chasing Jack down the eighteenth fairway, driver in hand. Fortunately (?) the tape ran out just at that point. Still, the Japanese got enough from network TV to pay for his trip to Miami.

Epilogue

Christmas morning—Four years later
Suburban Atlanta, The Peartree Home

To everyone's surprise, the marriage survived the honeymoon, and all the revelations that befell that event.

The twins are three years old. A striking black-haired little girl and a cherubic, dimpled blonde little boy. Jill, after maternity "leave" and two years nurturing the infants, is playing again, tuning up for another Georgia Ladies title. Jack, now a 2 handicapper, is determined to win his club championship, having missed by one stroke last year.

The family room floor is a varicolored mess; both children romp, lustily whooping, attired in feathered headdress, courtesy of their paternal grandparents. The Christmas tree lights sparkle, reflecting in Jill's eyes as she fondly surveys her husband and their brood. "The pail you fetched is running over, Jack," she proclaims.

His response is to sweep her off her feet, and twirl her wildly about, and he shouts, "I'd never have made it up the hill without you!"

The twins look at their parents in full embrace—little Robert looks at his sister and says, wisely, "Ecumenical!"

Golf is a harmonious subject in this household. She plays on Mondays, Wednesdays, and Fridays; he plays on Tuesdays, Saturdays, and Sundays—and as some great poet once wrote—"Never the twain will meet."

The Straw
or
The Old Man and the Mouse

He lived alone, in a ramshackle farmhouse, far up the hollow of his birth. He had been almost completely alone for several years now, since Sam had gone.

Once there had been a wife and a son, and later the daughter whose birth in the bedroom of that house had taken his wife away. He grieved and, after the grief diminished, he struggled to raise the crops and the son and the daughter.

As the years passed and the children became adults, he tilled the land, kept up the house and the barns, fished the streams and never complained. Always he taught them his personal credo—do not harm any living thing.

This lack of complaint was not in itself remarkable, since he seldom saw anyone except the mailman and neighbors, John and Mary Jordan, who lived across the creek, which flowed past the mouth of the hollow. What was remarkable was that he would not have complained had he lived in a crowded neighborhood.

The boy grew to manhood, joined the army and went to war; he returned in a coffin to be buried in the family cemetery. He laid the boy to rest under a huge beech tree that spread its foliage to shield the hillside cemetery plot. This time the grief lasted longer, and he found it much harder to keep his shoulders square. But he never complained.

The girl matured, fell in love with a construction

worker, and one day there was a note on the kitchen table saying, "Dear Daddy, Eddie and I are going to California. Love, Elizabeth."

Time passed and, after a year without further word from the girl, he was able to sleep better and accept that she was gone.

His name was Dan in keeping with his ancestry, since his maternal great grandfather was said to have been a close relative of Daniel Boone. In keeping with his lineage, he was very comfortable in the woods; or on the streams, and in the pioneer spirit, he kept to himself, for the most part.

Dan parted ways with his ancestors when it came to firearms. He owned no guns and never hunted, even though there were deer, rabbits, squirrels, grouse in abundance on his land.

His daily routine seldom varied: up at dawn, he cooked his solitary breakfast, firing up the kitchen wood stove immediately upon arising. After shaving and bathing, he set about the dozens of chores that he had carefully planned the night before. Shortly after ten each morning, he walked the mile to the foot of the hollow, crossed the seemingly precarious but actually very safe swinging bridge to the road and to his mailbox. He sat by the roadside and awaited his mail carrier, a Mr. Evans. Most days this was his only human contact, and since, most days, there was seldom any mail, it might have seemed an exercise in futility; but he always greeted the mailman cheerily and they talked about the weather, the crops, fishing, and politics.

Some days he carried chickens or vegetables or fruit to his friends, John and Mary Jordan, whose neat white house lay across the road from the mail box. Since they both worked in town, they had very little time for farming, but Mary kept Mr. Dan, as she called him, supplied with pies, cakes, and preserves.

Mary knew quite well of Mr. Dan's aversion to the killing of any living thing. She had once asked him to kill and dress a chicken; to her astonishment he grew red in the face, turned, and left without a word. Later she learned from the mailman that Mr. Dan never hunted, always released his fish unharmed, and shipped all his livestock rather than kill and butcher. Soft hearted and kind herself, she now felt an even greater sense of respect for her neighbor and friend. She knew of his losses, and she admired his stoicism and uncomplaining spirit.

"Sometimes, when I see him," said Mary to John, "I want to cry."

"Well," said John, "we know how his wife died, we've watched him lose his son, saw the girl move away, saw the old mare, Nellie, that carried the kids out of the bottom every morning, saw her die, and yet he has never uttered a word of complaint—well, we've got to try to do more for him—somehow we've got to do something to make his life a little more tolerable!"

So it was, that when their prize collie gave birth to a litter, the strongest and liveliest puppy was, when weaned, taken to Mr. Dan.

He named the dog Sam. He got Sam on his seventy-second birthday, and they were inseparable for almost ten years. Sam slept in Mr. Dan's bedroom, followed him in his daily chores, licked his hands and face, and in many ways became a part of the man. But Sam aged much faster than his owner, and lame and blind, Sam was pinned in a fence corner and gored by a young bull.

Sam was carefully carried up the hill, to rest forever alongside the wife and son. Mary wept bitterly, at least in part because Mr. Dan could not seem to do so.

The next several nights Dan slept fitfully. His only companion now was a little mouse that puttered across bedroom each evening. The mouse had not ventured out while Sam was in the room, but now emboldened, it skittered across the linoleum floor at all hours, and when Dan was aroused by the noise, he would throw a shoe at the little creature. He finally named the mouse "Nick," and after a few nights, he began to talk to the mouse, softly muttering imprecations, such as: "Get back to bed, Nick," or "I'm gonna break your little gray back," or "Nick, I'll swear, if you wake me up one more time, I'm gonna let you have it!"

Perhaps, even a mouse could recognize these as idle threats. Certainly anyone who knew Dan would have known they were false. So, once again Dan had an object on which to bestow his affection.

"John," said Mary one night, "next Tuesday is his eighty-second birthday. Why don't we get all his friends and neighbors and have a surprise birthday party?"

"Mary, you are a genius," said John. "I'll start calling right now." And so it was that three days later Mr. Dan and Mr. Evans (a co-conspirator) went fishing, and when they tied up the boat beneath the swinging bridge, the mail man insisted upon walking his friend home, using the pretext of needing some apples.

Mr. Dan was completely surprised and seemingly delighted to find his yard full of automobiles, horses, and even a buggy. There were festively dressed people on the porch, and swinging in his porch swing.

Mary had placed a bright red gingham table cloth on the porch table, and the table was laden with food. There were presents piled shoulder high in the living room, and several ladies presided over the old wood stove, frying chickens, making gravy, and baking biscuits. As his friend greeted Mr. Dan, Mary saw that he was thoroughly delighted with the surprise party.

Mary also saw that Mr. Dan was most delighted to

greet Mrs. Walker, a fiftyish buxom, handsome widow. Dan insisted upon carrying their plates to the yard table and sat beside her during the dinner hour.

Mary, with emotions she could never have explained, was somewhat chagrined when Dan arose by placing his hands, almost too casually, on the widow's bare shoulder. Mrs. Walker beamed and fluttered lashes like a starlet.

The presents were opened and ranged from a pair of stylish jeans to a new shovel. There were numerous boxes of candy, a fruit cake, and last, by careful planning, a gallon of crystal-clear liquid.

Dan, urged by Mr. Evans and others, took first sip, then a swig, and finally almost half a glassful. A fiddle appeared and then another, and soon the yard came alive to country music and square dancing. There were almost two hours of frenetic gaiety, and then almost as if by common accord, the activities ceased and the party was over.

It was time for good-byes and final Happy Birthdays, but perhaps not too strangely, both Dan and the Widow Walker were missing. At first Mary was peeved, but the more she thought about it, the more she felt happy for Mr. Dan.

Dan went to bed, still feeling the effects of the moonshine, but by no means inebriated. Instead, his thoughts seemed very clear, and he was looking forward to tomorrow, when Mrs. Walker had promised to return. He was supposed to help her string beans, something he had done for many many years.

He locked the bedroom door as he had done for decades, even though he had always known that there would not be an intruder. He sat on the edge of the bed, slipped out of pants and shirt, and took off a shoe. Nick ran out of his crevice, skittering across the floor. Dan grinned, saying, "Get back in your hole, critter" and tossed his shoe at the little mouse. The heavy shoe flew in an arc and landed heel first squarely on Nick's little head. The mouse lay still. Dan leaped from the bed and ran to the deathly still creature. "Oh, Nick, Nick!" he shouted. "What have I done?"

Almost a month passed before Dr. Baker, the county coroner, reviewed a report from the state medical examiner. After the usual salutations, the examiner went on to say "I'm sorry to tell you that I have been unable to determine a 'cause of death' for this old gentleman. His organ systems were all normal and functional. More especially, there was nothing in the heart, the brain, or the cardiovascular system to pinpoint the cause of death. Indeed his anatomic and physiological findings were those of a much younger person. Toxicology screens were negative, and there were no signs of trauma. I'm not attempting any levity when I say that all of organ systems were in great shape and were functional since we found semen in his clothing, indicating that he had engaged in some form of sexual activity shortly before his death. I can only postulate that some type of cardiac arrhythmia occurred, due to sudden release of catecholamines. This could occur from great elation, great excitement, or great sorrow; or perhaps some combination of these."

By coincidence, John Jordan was talking to Mary at the same time Dr. Baker read the examiner's report.

"I really think old Dan died from a heart attack, Mary. When I finally broke into the bedroom, he was lying flat on his back, he still had his underwear and one shoe on, and he had his right hand over his heart."

"I guess you are right, dear," said Mary. "That would certainly suggest he was having pain in his chest."

Only one thing I can't understand though," mused John, "in his hand, pressed against his heart, was this little gray mouse."

A Message from Dayle

Hi, I'm a dog, my name is Dayle. I live with a cranky old man in a huge somewhat run-down old house. We live back in the hills, deep in the woods, alongside a lake.

I've been told I'm descended from a great line of hunting dogs, which once served the royal rulers of a place in Europe, called Weimar. This, then, makes me a Weimaraner. I have a doghouse, but since my ancestors lived in a castle, I refuse to use it. I will sleep in the old man's bedroom, however, since he has a pair of bedroom slippers that are very comfortable—to chew on. It's somewhat difficult to live with the old man. He is irritable and sometimes refuses to pay attention when I bark a command. He does put out food for me twice a day, but since my forefathers lived on deer meat, and pheasants, I eat this repulsive dry food only when I'm desperate.

He drives away, every morning, leaving me in charge of the home, forest, and lake, but he leaves me alone in the wilderness, and so most times, I try to follow him. His old van will scarcely make it over the hill road that leads out to civilization, and I can outrun it easily, but when I do he becomes angry and hateful then usually gets out a leash. When he approaches with the leash, I know he is going to tie me up to a tree, so I run back to our humble home, at least there, water is plentiful, and I may catch a ground squirrel, or a mouse, or find a dead limb to chew.

Sometimes, I almost feel sorry for my cranky old keeper. He gets this tuft of fur that stands straight up on the back of his head. I've tried licking it when he's asleep, but he wakes up and swats me across my rear end. He just doesn't seem to appreciate what I do for him. He's also got this weird habit. He gets into a long box that floats and goes around the lake carrying a long, slender black stick, and a piece of line. Sometimes a foolish fish will jump up and bite the end of the line and then the crazy old man jerks and pulls until he gets the fish to the box, and then, guess what? He holds the fish in his hand, talks to it, and then throws it back. Why would anyone talk to a fish? Well, sure, I bark sometimes, but that's so they'll know I'm the boss. People sure are weird!

Occasionally we have visitors, who usually come to fish in our lake. Some are successful; especially if they pay attention to me, when I try to show them, by wading or swimming, where the fish are hiding.

I'd be happy to have you come visit me. Just sign on to www.(this stands for Wild Weinmaraner in Wilderness) Dayle.com and I'll send you directions. Woof!